A Color of His Own

To Vera Barbara

Leo Lionni

A Color of His Own

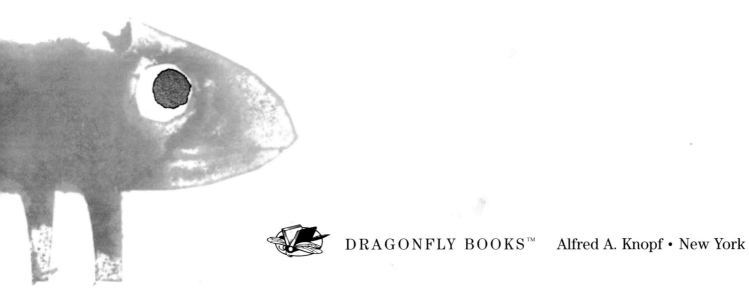

DRAGONFLY BOOKS™   Alfred A. Knopf • New York

Parrots are green

goldfish are red

elephants are gray

pigs are pink.

All animals have a color of their own—

except for chameleons.

They change color wherever they go.

On lemons they are yellow.

In the heather they are purple.

And on the tiger they are striped
like tigers.

One day a chameleon
who was sitting
on a tiger's tail
said to himself,

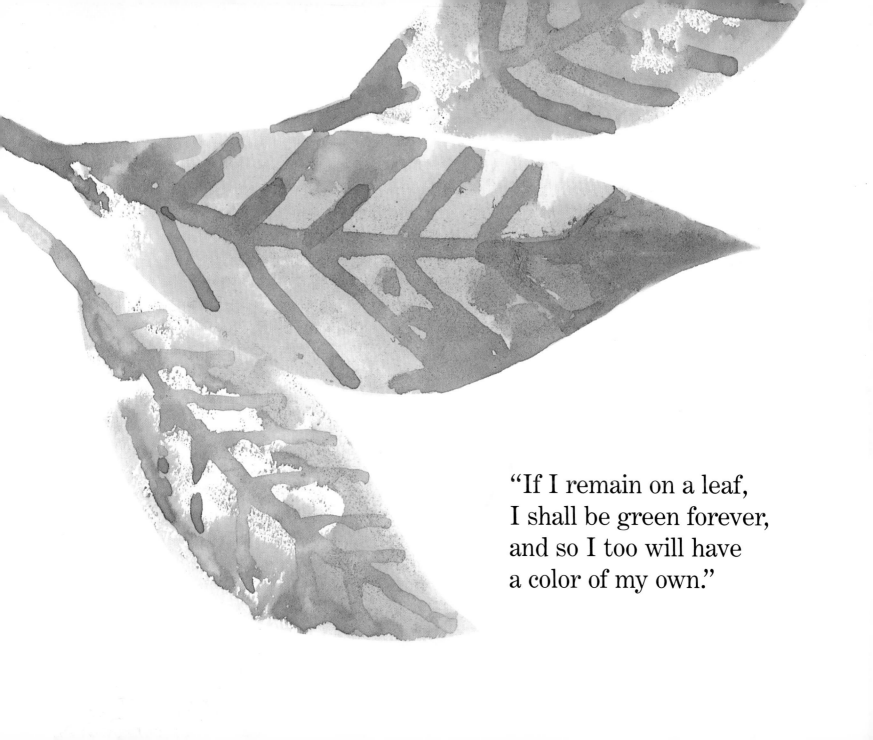

"If I remain on a leaf,
I shall be green forever,
and so I too will have
a color of my own."

With this thought he cheerfully climbed
onto the greenest leaf.

But in autumn the leaf turned yellow
—and so did the chameleon.

Later the leaf turned red,
and the chameleon too turned red.

And then
the winter winds
blew the leaf from
the branch
and with it
the chameleon.

The chameleon was black in the long winter night.

But when spring came, he walked out
into the green grass.
And there he met another chameleon.

He told his sad story.
"Won't we ever have a color
of our own?" he asked.

"I'm afraid not," said the other chameleon,
who was older and wiser.
"But," he added,
"why don't we stay together?

"We will still change color
wherever we go,
but you and I
will always be alike."

And so they remained side by side.

They were green together

and purple

and yellow

and red with white polka dots. And they lived happily

DRAGONFLY BOOKS™ PUBLISHED BY ALFRED A. KNOPF, INC.

Copyright © 1975 by Leo Lionni.
All rights reserved under International and Pan-American Copyright Conventions. Published in the United States by
Alfred A. Knopf, Inc., New York, and simultaneously in Canada by Random House of Canada Limited, Toronto.
Distributed by Random House, Inc., New York. Published in hardcover by Pantheon Books, a division of Random
House, Inc., in 1975. Originally published in Great Britain by Abelard-Schuman Limited in 1975.

http://www.randomhouse.com/

Library of Congress Cataloging-in-Publication Data
Lionni, Leo. A color of his own.
British ed. published in 1975 under title: A colour of his own.
Summary: A little chameleon is distressed that he doesn't have his own color like other animals.
[1. Chameleons—Fiction] I. Title.
PZ7.L6634Co3   [E]   75-28456

ISBN 0-679-88785-7 (pbk.)

First Dragonfly Books™ edition: September 1997

Printed in the United States of America

10 9 8 7 6 5 4 3 2